Mr. Dryden, John Fletcher

The Pilgrim A Comedy

In Five Acts

Mr. Dryden, John Fletcher

The Pilgrim A Comedy
In Five Acts

ISBN/EAN: 9783744776820

Printed in Europe, USA, Canada, Australia, Japan

Cover: Foto ©Andreas Hilbeck / pixelio.de

More available books at **www.hansebooks.com**

THE

PILGRIM.

A

COMEDY.

IN FIVE ACTS.

Written originally

By *FLETCHER.*

Afterwards altered

By *DRYDEN.*

Now Revived, with Material ADDITIONS, and Printed under
the Inspection of JAMES WRIGHTEN, Prompter.

EXACTLY AGREEABLE TO THE REPRESENTATION

AT THE

Theatre-Royal in Drury-Lane.

For W. LOWNDES, No. 77, Fleet-street.
MDCCLXXXVII.

PRICE ONE SHILLING.

In Octavo, Price 1s. each, sewed.

1. SEEING IS BELIEVING, a dramatic Proverb of one Act, written by Paul Joddrel, Esq. as performed at the Theatre Royal in the Haymarket.

2. Embellished with a beautiful and animated Portrait of Mrs. JORDAN, drawn from Life by Stothard, and elegantly engraved by Angus, THE ROMP, a Musical Entertainment of two Acts, altered from Love in the City, by 'Mr. Bickerstaff, as acted at all the Theatres Royal.

3. Ornamented with a striking Likeness of Mrs. BROWN, taken from Life by Stothard, and correctly engraved by Scott, THE VIRGIN UNMASKED, a Musical Entertainment, in one Act, altered from Fielding, as represented at the Theatres Royal in Drury-Lane, and Covent-Garden.

4. Illustrated with a neat characteristic Frontispiece, by those eminent Artists Dodd and Collyer, THE COUNTRY WIFE, a Farce in two Acts, altered from Wycherly, and performed at the Theatre Royal in Covent-Garden.

And also in Octavo, Price 1s. 6d. sewed,

5. Enriched with a capital full length Portrait of Mr. EDWIN, in the Character of Jerry Blackacre, accurately drawn from Life in a masterly Manner by Ryley, and engraved in a superior Stile by Angus, THE PLAIN DEALER, a Comedy in five Acts, altered from Wycherly by Mr. Bickerstaff, as it is performed at the Theatre Royal in Covent-Garden.

Soon will be published, a new Edition of

SHE WOULD AND SHE WOULD NOT, a Comedy in five Acts, written by C. Cibber; with Alterations, as now performed at the Theatre Royal in Drury-Lane, adorned by a Portrait of Mrs. JORDAN, taken from Life, with Permission, by Stothard, and engraved by Sharp.

Dramatis Personæ.

M E N.

Pedro (the Pilgrim),		Mr. KEMBLE.
Alphonso,	—	Mr. BADDELEY.
Roderigo,	—	Mr. BARRYMORE.
Curio,	—	Mr. STAUNTON.
Seberto,	—	Mr. WILLIAMES.
Governor of Segovia,		Mr. PHILLIMORE.
Old Pilgrim,	—	Mr. PACKER.
Lopez,	—	Mr. SUETT.
Jaquez,	—	Mr. BURTON.
Stuttering Servant,		Mr. R. PALMER.
Drunken Servant,		Mr. BATES.
Porter,	—	Mr. FAWCETT.
Gentlemen,	— {	Messrs. WILSON, and BENSON.
Outlaws,	— }	Messrs. SPENCER, ALFRED, and LYONS.
Mad Scholar,	—	Mr. WHITFIELD.
Mad Englishman,		Mr. R. PALMER.
Mad Taylor,	—	Mr. WALDRON.
Master of Madhouse,		Mr. CHAPLIN.
Keepers of ditto,	{	Messrs. FAWCETT and JONES.
Peasants,	— }	Messrs. LAMASH, BATES, and PHILLIMORE.
Beggars,	— }	Messrs. JONES and LYONS.

W O M E N.

Alinda,	—	Mrs. TAYLOR.
A Fool,	—	Miss COLLINS.
And Juletta,	—	Mrs. JORDAN.

The PILGRIM.

ACT I. SCENE I. *A Room in Alphon-
so's House.

Enter Alphonso, Curio, *and* Seberto.

Cur. SIGNIOR Alphonso, you are too rugged
with her, too harsh; indeed you are.

Alph. Yes, it seems so.

Seb. A father of so sweet a child, so good, so
beautiful; fie, sir, fie, so excellent a creature.

Alph. She's a fool; away.

Seb. Can you be angry? Can any wind blow
rough upon a blossom so fair and tender? Can a
father's nature, a noble father's too?

Alph. All this is but prating: Let her be ruled;
let her observe my humour; with my eyes let her
see; with my ears let her hear; I am her father;
I begat her; I bred her, and by Jupiter I will—

Seb. No doubt you may compel her, but think
how wretched you by force may make her.

Alph. Wretched! wretched! is't not a man I
force her to? A noble man; a rich man; a handsome man; a young man; a strong man; none
of your pieced companions, none of your washy
rogues, that fly to fritters upon every puff of weather. I force her to a strong dog, don't I? What
would the flirt have?

Seb. I grant you, Roderigo is all these, and a
brave gentleman: But does it therefore follow she
must doat upon him? Will you allow no liberty
in chusing?

B   *Cur.*

Cur. Alas she's tender yet.

Alph. Tough, tough, tough as the devil; you see I can't break her.

Seb. You put her to too hard a trial : you know though he has merit, he's a banish'd man, an out-law; you know the life he leads; that he's the head of a rough band of robbers; judge what ef-fect his bloody rapines must needs ere this, have work'd upon his nature. A rugged mate, I doubt, for such a dove.

Cur. Rugged indeed; such different tempers, where can you ever hope to reconcile ?

Alph. Rugged ! she'll find ways to soften him. And for the pranks he plays in's banishment, it shews he's a mettled fellow : he'll make 'em weary o' their sentence; a small composition will restore him. But I know the secret of all this : my minx has some other in view; some flickering slave or other, some sweet-scented coxcomb, that——a ——sings, I'll warrant you, and ——a——lutes it, languishes, and has no beard; ha ! is't not so ?

Seb. So far from what you charge her with, I would engage my life, she has not yet a glance to answer for.

Cur. I never yet beheld more modesty.

Seb. Nor I, in one so young, so much discre-tion.

Alph. ——Hum——and yet there was a fellow (dead I hope) whom I have seen her glance at, till I thought the hussy would have stuck her eyes into the rascal.

Seb. Pray, who was that ?

Alph. Pedro, sir, only Pedro, old Fernando's hopeful heir; my mortal foe, whose family I wish confumed; that's all, sir.

Seb. If that be all, you have nothing left to
fear;

fear; for Pedro, urged by secret discontent, has left his father, friends, and all; and, as 'tis said, is gone to range the world.

Alph. With all my heart. He was a beggar, so strolling is his business.

Cur. He was a beggar, but a noble beggar; shame on the court for suffering him to be so.

Alph. Shame on those who encourage beggars, I say. Here's this young slut, in the midst of her rebellion, is so very religious, she undoes me with her charity. Why, what a crew of vermin have I about my door every day to receive meat, drink, and money from her fair hands. Not a rogue that can say his prayers, groan, and turn his pipe to lamentation, but she thinks she's bound to dance to.

Enter Alinda *and* Juletta.

Alph. O, are you there, mistress? Well, how goes disobedience to-day?—That's a base, down look—Ah you sturdy young jade.

Cur. Pray, be more gentle to her.

Alph. Pray be quiet; I know best how to deal with her: and I will make her obey, or I will make her——

Alin. Sir, you may make me any thing; you know I'm all obedience, there's nothing but my prayers and tears oppose you.

Alph. Then will I oppose nothing but your prayers and tears. Now I hope you can't complain of me.

Cur. Poor lady, how I pity her!

Alph. Pray keep your pity for a better occasion. Look you, gentlewoman, you know my will; and, in that, you know all: so I leave you, to digest it; and I desire these gentlemen will do so too.

[*Exit* Alphonso.

Cur. A better hour attend you, madam.

Alin. I thank ye, gentlemen:

[*Exeunt Cur. and Seb.*

Alas! I want such comforts. Would I could thank you too, father; but your cruelty won't give me leave. Grant, heaven, I mayn't forget my duty to him.

Jul. If you do, madam, heaven will forgive you for't, ne'er fear it. A perverse old fool!

[*Aside.*

Alin. What poor attend my charity to-day, Juletta?

Jul. Enough of all forts, madam; some that deserve your pity, some that don't; but I wish you would be merry with your charity; a chearful look becomes it.

Alin. Alas! Juletta, what is there for me to be merry at? What joy have I in view?

Jul. Joy; why what joy, i'th name of wonder, would you have, but a husband? A handsome young fellow, who'll send your spleen to the devil, madam.

Alin. Away, light fool; I doubt there's poor contentment to be found in marriage. Yet could I find a man——

Jul. You may a thousand.

Alin. Meer men, I know I may. But such a man, from whose example (as from a compass) we may steer our course, and safe arrive at such a memory as shall become our ashes; such men are rare indeed. But no more of this; 'tis not discourse that's suited to thy giddy temper: let's go and see what poor afflicted wretches want my charity. [*Exeunt.*

SCENE

SCENE II.

The Porch of Alphonso's *House.*

Porter, Beggars, Pedro *and an old* Pilgrim, *discovered.*

Port. Stand off, and keep your ranks. Twenty-foot-farther.——The sun shines warm. The farther still the better.

1st Beg. Hey ho ! heav'n bless our mistress.

Port. Does the crack go that way, old hunger, ha ? 'Twill be o' my side anon.

2d Beg. Bray, friend, be kind to us.

Port. Friend ! your friend ; and why your friend, sirrah, meagre chaps ? What do you see in me, or without me, ha ! that I should be your friend ? This young soft-hearted mistress of mine does make these rogues so familiar.

2d Beg. I'm sure I would be your worship's friend.

Port. No doubt on't, sirrah ! any man's friend for what you can get.

1st Beg. I'm sure it's twelve o'clock.

Port. 'Tis ever so with thee, when thou hast done scratching ; for that provokes thy stomach to ring noon. O the infinite seas of porridge thou hast swallowed ! alms do you call it, to relieve these rascals ?

Enter Alphonso, Curio, and Seberto.

Alph. Look you there ! Did not I tell you how she would undoe me ! What marts of rogues and beggars !

Seb. 'Tis charity methinks you are bound to love her for.

Alph. Yes, I'll warrant you. If men could sail to heaven in porridge-pots, with masts of beef and
mutton,

mutton, what a voyage fhould I make ! What are
all thefe here ?

1ſt Beg. Poor people, an't like your worſhip.

2d Beg. Wretched poor people.

All. Very hungry people.

Alph. And very louſy. And what are you?
(*to the Pilg.*)

Old Pilg. Strangers, that come to wonder at
your charity ; yet people poor enough to beg a
bleſſir.g.

Cur. Uſe 'em gently, fir. they have a reverend
mein.   You are holy pilgrims, are you not ?

Old Pilg. We are, fir, and bound far off, to
offer our devotions.

Alph. What do you do here then ? We have no
reliques, no holy ſhrines.

Old Pilg. The holieſt we ever heard of : you
keep a living monument of goodneſs ; a daughter
of that pious excellence, the very ſhrines of faints
fink at her virtue.   We come to fee this lady; not
with profane eyes or wanton blood, to doat upon her beauty ; but through our tedious way; to
beg her bleſſing.

Alph. This is a new way of begging; thefe com-
mendations cry money for reward, good ſtore too:
Ah ! the fainting of this young harlot will coſt me
dear.

(*To Pedro*) Well fir, have you got your com-
pliments ready too, and your empty purfe ? Ha !
what nothing but a bow, modeſty ?

Cur. A handfome well-look'd man. (*afide*)

Alph. What country craver are you ? What !
nothing but motion ? A puppit pilgrim.

Old Pilg. He's a ftranger, fir ; thefe four days
I have travel'd in his company, but little of his
bufinefs or his language yet I have underſtood.

Seb.

Seb. Both young and handsome; only the sun has injured him.

Alph. Would you have money, sir, or meat, or a wench? What kind of blessing does your devotion point at? Still more ducking! Are there any saints that understand by sign only? Hah, more motion yet? This is the prettiest pilgrim; the pink of pilgrims.

Cur. Fie, sir, fie; rather bestow your charity than jest upon him.

Alph. Say you so? Why then look ye, pilgrim, here's a poor *viaticum*, very good gold, sir, I'm sorry 'tis not heavier. But since the lightest grain of earthy dross would be a burden to a heavenly mind——I'll put it up again.

Cur. O horrible! you are too irreverent.

Alph. You are a fool. Must I give my money to every rogue that carries a grave look in's face? Must my good angels wait upon him? I'll find 'em other business.

Seb. But consider, sir, the wrong you do those men may light on you: strangers are entitled to a softer usage.

Alph. Oons, half the kingdom will be strangers shortly, if this young slut's suffer'd to go on with her prodigalities. But I must be an ass: Here, sirrah, (*to Porter*) see 'em relieved for once; do't effectually too; d'ye hear? Burst 'em, that I may never see 'em more. [*Exit Alphonso.*

Cur. Such a face as that, sure I have seen.

Seb. I thought so too; but we must be mistaken. [*Exeunt Curio and Seberto.*

Port. Come, will ye troop up, porridge regiment? Captain *Poor-Quarter*, will ye move?

Enter

Enter Alinda *and* Juletta.

Alin. Why are not thefe poor wretches ferved yet?

All Beg. Blefs our good miftrefs.

Port. They are too high fed, madam, their ftomachs are not awake yet.

Alin. Do you make fport with their miferies? fir, learn more humanity, or I fhall find a way to teach it you.

1ft Beg. Kind heaven preferve her, and for ever blefs her.

Alin. Blefs the good end that I mean it for.

[*Exeunt Porter and Beggars.*

Jul. (*afide*) Would I knew what that were; if it be for a man, I'd fay *amen* with all my heart.— You have a very pretty band of penfioners, madam.

Alin. Vain-glory would feek more and handfomer; but I appeal to virtue what my end is.— What men are thefe?

Jul. Holy pilgrims they feem to be. What pity 'tis that handfome young fellow fhould undergo fo much penance: Would I were the faint he makes his vow to; I'd foon grant his requeft, let him afk what he would.

Alin. You are pilgrims, firs, is't not fo?

Old Pilg. We are, fair faint; may heaven's grace furround you; may all good thoughts and prayers dwell about you; abundance be your friend, and holy charity be ever at your hand to crown you glorious.

Alin. I than you, fir, peace guide your travels too; and, what you wifh for moft, end all your troubles. Remember me by this (*giving him money*), and in your prayers, when your ftrong heart melts, meditate my poor fortunes.

Old

Old Pilg. All my devotions wait upon your service.

Alin. Are you of this country, fir?

Old Pilg. Yes, worthieft lady, but far off bred: My fortune's farther from me.

Alin. I am no inquifitor; whatever vow, or penance pulls you on, fir, confcience, or love, or ftubborn difobedience, the faint you kneel to, hear and eafe your travels.

Old Pilg. Yours ne'er begin; and thus I feal my prayers. [*Exit.*

Alin. (*afide*) How ftedfaftly this man looks up-on me! How he fighs! Some great affliction fure's the fource of his devotions.

(*To Pedro.*) Right holy fir. He turns from us: Alas he weeps too: Something preffes him he would reveal, but dares not. Sir, be comforted: If you want, to me you appear fo worthy of relief, I'll be your fteward. Speak and take. He's dumb ftill! This man affects me ftrangely!

Jul. I like his fhape well. (*afide*)

Alin. It may be he would fpeak to me alone. (*afide*) Retire a little, Julietta; but d'ye hear, don't be far off.

Jul. I fhan't, madam: Would I were nearer him: A young, fmug, handfome holinefs has no fellow. (*afide*) [*Retires.*

Alin. Why do you grieve? Do you find your penance fharp? Are the vows you have made too mighty for you? Or does the world allure you to look back, and make you mourn the fofter hours you have loft? You are young, and feem as you were form'd for manly refolution: Come, be comforted.

Ped. I am, fair angel: and fuch a comfort from your words I feel, that tho' calamities like angry

waves,

waves, curl round, contending proudly who shall first devour me, yet I will stem their danger.

Alin. He speaks nobly.   (*aside*)
What do you want, sir ?

Ped. All that can make me happy : I want myself.

Alin. Yourself! who robb'd you, pilgrim ?
Why does he look so earnestly upon me ?
I want myself !
Indeed you holy wanderers are said to seek much:
But to seek yourselves ———

Ped. I *seek myself, and am but myself's shadow,*
have lost myself, and now am not so noble.

Alin. (*aside*) I seek myself ! Sure, something I
remember bears that motto ; it is not he ; he's
younger, has a smother face ; yet for that *self* sake,
pilgrim, whosoe'er it be, take this. (*offers money*)

Ped. Your hand I dare take ; that be far from
me : Your hand I hold, and thus I kiss it ; and
thus I bless it too. *Be constant still : Be good : And
live to be a great example.*   [*Exit.*

Alin. One word more. He's gone : Heav'n,
how I tremble ! *Be constant still* ; 'tis the very
posy here ; and here without, *be good.* He wept
too as he left me. It must be Pedro. Juletta.

Juletta *comes forward.*

Jul. Madam.
Alin. Take this key, and quickly fetch me the
jewel that lies in my little cabinet. (*Exit Juletta*)
That will determine all. It must be he : His face
was smoother when I saw him last ; yett here's
a manly look, a noble shape, still speak him
Pedro.

Enter Juletta.

Alin. Let me see it : 'Tis so ; 'tis he ; it must
be he : He spoke the words just as they stand en-

graven here. *I seek myself and am but myself's shadow.* Poor Pedro! But how shall I recover him? Juletta, the pilgrim, where is he? Which way did he go?

Jul. Alas! madam, I don't know; it's in vain to seek him now.

Alin. I tell thee I must see him; I gave him nothing.

Jul. That was ill done, indeed; for he's the handsomest fellow I have seen this many a day. What makes her look so thoughtful? Sure here's something afoot more than ordinary. *Exit.*

Alin. 'Tis enough. He has done much for me: I'll try what recompence 'tis in my power to make him.

Forgive me, duty, if I break thy laws!
My father's harsh and bitter treatment
Makes me renounce my home—home I have none
Without the youth I love—Oh Pedro!
Thro' ev'ry change of fortune I will fly,
Thro' all inclemencies of earth and sky,
The sharpest trials of my fortunes prove,
To follow, and reward my constant love. [*Exit.*

End of Act I.

A C T   II.

S C E N E I. *A Room in* Alphonso's *House.*

Enter Alphonso, Curio, Seberto, Juletta, *Porter and Servants.*

Alph. CAN she slip through a key-hole? Tell me that, resolve me: Can she fly i'th' air? Is she invisible? Gone, and no body knew it!

Seb. Pray be more moderate.

Alph. 'Oons find her out, or I'll hang ye all; you wagtail, you know her defigns, you were of her council, (*to Jul.*) her advifer ; where is fhe, huffy ?

Jul. You would know of me, fir ?

Alph. Of you, fir ! Yes of you, fir ; why what are you, fir ?

Jul. Her fervant, fir, her faithful fervant.

Alph. Servant ! her fiddle-ftick, her lady fairy, to oil the doors o'nights, that they mayn't creak. Where is fhe, infamy ?

Jul. 'Tis very well.

Alph. You lye, 'tis ill, damnable ill ; and either confefs, or———

Jul. Indeed I won't.

Seb. Why ?

Jul. Becaufe I can't ; if I could, I'd give another reafon.

Alph. Well faid ; but I fhall deal with you, you flut you. What fay you, thick-fkull, which way did fhe get out ! Why were not my doors fhut ? (*to the Porter*)

Port. They were an't pleafe you ; nothing open but the key-hole.

Alph. Where did fhe lie ; who lay with her ?

Port. Not I, an't pleafe you ; I lay with Frederick in the flea-chamber.

Alph. Once more, of thee I demand her ; tell me news of her, or expect———the devil and all.

(*to Juletta*)

Cur. Come, Juletta, if you know any thing, tell him———

Jul. Look ye, fir, if I knew all, and had been intrufted by her, not all the devils, you could call upon, fhould fcare one fingle hint from me.

But,

But, fince I know nothing worth your knowing,
I'll tell you what I do know.   I know fhe's gone,
becaufe we can't find her.   I know fhe's gone
cunningly, becaufe you can't find which way.   I
know fhe was weary of your tyranny, becaufe the
devil would have been fo too: And I know, if
fhe's wife, fhe'll never come again——

Alph. Out of my doors.

Jul. That's all my poor petition.   For were
your houfe gold, and fhe not in't, I fhould think
it but a cage to whiftle in.

Alph. Jade ; if fhe be above ground, I'll have
her—

Jul. I'd live in a coal-pit then, if I were fhe.

Cur. Indeed, fir, I fancy fhe knows nothing of
her flight ; you know her mad way of talking.

Alph. Hang her, hang her, fhe knows too much.

Enter Servant drunk.

Well, rafcal, have you any news of her ?

Serv. N—N—Not a drop, fir :   The butler
gave me the key of the cellar, to fearch the cellar,
fir; fo I have been fearching the cellar.

Alph. Here's a dog for you.

Serv. I fearch'd every hogfhead, fir, and open'd
fome bottles, but could not find a fpoonful of her.

Alph. You rafcal, get you out of my reach, or
I'll be thy murderer: [*Servant retires.*

Enter another Servant that ftammers.

Serv. S, S, S, S, Sir.

Alph. Well, what news ?   Be quick.

Serv. My yo, yo, yo, yo, young la-day is gone—

Alph. I know fhe's gone, you dog ; but where ?

Serv. Out at the P——

Alph. Out with't, you fon of a whore——

Serv. The Po, ho, ho, ho, ho, hoftern gate of
the ga, ha, ha, ha ——

Alph. This dog will make me mad; but one
ftammering rogue in the family, and it muft fall

to his fhare to give me an account of her. The wind's in the Eaft too: the dog won't get it out this hour. Where was it, firrah! where was it?

Serv. The ga-arden, fir, the ga-arden.

Alph. The garden, fir, the garden; was it fo? And how do you know fhe got out of the garden, ha?

Serv. I f—— f—— faw, an't p, p, p, p, p-leafe you, the p——— print of her fo, fo, fo, foot.

Alph. Right, a foot, a little foot, a young whore's foot?

Serv. Yes, fir.

Alph. And from thence fcrambled over the wall into the park, and fo to the devil?

Serv. So I fup,-p,-pofe, fir.——   [*retires up.*

Alph. 'Tis very well, ye ftars, 'tis very well: this comes of indulgence, I muft needs allow her the key of the garden, to walk on faft-days, and contemplate, with a pox: but I'll fetch her again, with a firebrand at her tail. My horfes there.——

Cur. You'll give us leave to wait upon you?

Alph. That you may, if you pleafe. My horfe there; difpatch. Are you fo hot? I'faith, I'll cool you, miftrefs: muft you be jumping Joan? If I catch you again, I'll clap fuch a clog about your neck, you fhall leap no more walls, I'll warrant you; I'll hang Roderigo there, I'faith. My horfes, quick; and d'ye hear, keep me this young lirry poop within doors, faft; I fhall difcover dame——   [*Exeunt Alphonfo, Curio, and Seberto.*

Stam. Serv. He's in the devil of a paffion,

[*Exeunt Servants.*

Jul. Indeed you won't, difcover fir. Well, love, if thou be'ft with her; or whatever power elfe arms her refolution, conduct her carefully, and keep her from this madman—Direct her to her wifhes; dwell about her, let no difhonourable end o'ertake her, danger or want; and let me try my fortune———

S O N G:

THIS hot purſuit,
  With threats to boot,
     Have little to alarm me,
So war I wage,
Defy his rage,
     And brave whate'er may harm me,

He ſtill may ſwear,
And ſtamp and ſtare,
     I'll neither fear nor faulter,
Whate'er may bind,
'Gainſt woman's mind,
     Will prove a rotten halter.

My miſtreſs flown,
I'll ſoon be gone ;——
     Old cruſty ſwears he'll tame her ;
For him ſhe loves,
Abroad ſhe roves
     In truth I cannot blame her.

In varied ſhapes,
Thro' hair-breadth ſcapes,
     Each way he tries to win her :
She ſcorns reſtraint,
And ſuch a ſaint,
     Would make e'en me a ſinner.

Some trim diſguiſe,
No doubt ſhe tries,
     I'll follow her example :
Of faith, of ſkill,
And wit at will,
     I'll give 'em ſtraight a ſample.

So ſhe and I
Will fairly try,
     Whoſe trick or change can blind moſt ;
And ſince old Don,
You chuſe to run,
     The devil take the hindmoſt,   [Exit.

S C E N E II.   *A Foreſt and Cave.*

Enter Roderigo *and Out-laws.*

1ſt Out. You are not merry, captain.

Rod. Why, we get nothing, we have no ſport: wenching and drinking ſpoil us; we keep no guard.

2d Out. I'm ſure there's neither merchant nor gentleman paſſes, but we have tribute.

Rod. Yes, and while we ſpend that idly, we let thoſe paſs that carry the beſt booty: I'll have all ſearch'd and brought in. Rogues and beggars have found the trick of late to become bankers. In ſhort, gentlemen, I'll have none eſcape but my friends and neighbours, who may be uſeful in laying my innocence before the king: all others ſhall pay their paſſport.

2d Out. You now ſpeak like a captain; if we ſpare any, flea us, and coin our caſſocks.

Rod. You hear of no preparations the king in-tends againſt us?

1ſt Out. Not a word: don't we ſe chis garriſons?

Rod. Who have we out now?

2d Out. Good fellows, that, if there be any purchaſe ſtirring, won't ſlip it; Jaques and Lopez, lads that know their buſineſs.

Rod. Where's the boy you brought in e'en now? He's a pretty lad, and of a quick capacity——

1ſt Out. He's within at meat, ſir; the poor knave's hungry; yet he ſeaſons all he eats or drinks, with tears.

2d Out. He's young; 'tis fear and want of company.

Rod:

Rod. Don't ufe him roughly, and he'll foon grow bolder. I intend to keep him to wait upon me; I like the boy; there's fomething in his face pleafes me ftrangely: be fure you all ufe him gently.

1ft Out. Here's a little box, fir, we took about him, which almoft broke his heart to part with: I fancy there's fomething of value in it; I can't open it.

Rod. Alas! fome little money, I warrant you, the poor knave carry'd to defray his charge: I'll give it him again.

Enter Jaques, Lopez, *and Outlaws, with* Pedro. How now! Who's this? What have you brought me here, foldiers?

Jaq. Why, truly, we don't well know; only he's a damn'd fullen fellow.

Rod. Where did you take him?

Lop. Upon the fkirt of the wood, fauntering and peeping about, as if he were looking for the beft accefs to our quarters: money he had enough; and, when we threatened him, he fmiled and yielded, but would not fpeak one word.

Rod. Pilgrim, come hither; are you a pilgrim, fir? A piece of pretty holinefs; do you fhrink, my mafter? A fmug young faint this. What country were you born in, I pray? What, not a word? Had your mother this excellent virtue too? Sure, fhe was a matchlefs woman: what a bleffed family this fellow fprung from! fure he was begot in a calm. Are your lips fealed, or do you fcorn to anfwer? Look you, fir, you are in my hands; and I fhall be too hard for you: put off his bon-net, foldiers. You have a fpeaking face, fir.

Lop. A handfome one, I'm fure; this pilgrim can't want fhe-faints to pray to.

D   *Rod.*

Rod. Stand nearer: ha?

Ped. Come, do your worſt; I am ready.

Rod. Have you found your tongue then? Retire all, and let me talk with him alone; and keep your guards ſtrict. (*Exeunt all but Rod. and Ped.*) So, now, what art thou?

Ped. What am I? My habit ſhews me what I am.

Rod. A deſperate fool; and ſo thy fate ſhall tell thee. What devil brought thee hither? For I know thee.

Ped. I know thou doſt; and ſince it is my fortune to light into thy hands, I muſt conclude the moſt malicious of devils brought me; yet ſome men ſay thou art noble——

Rod. Not to thee; that were a benefit to mock the giver. Thy father hates my friends and family; and thou haſt been the heir of all his malice: can two ſuch ſtorms then meet, and part without kiſſing?

Ped. You have the mightier hand.

Rod. And ſo I'll uſe it.

Ped. I cannot hinder you; leſs can I beg ſubmiſſive at his knees that knows no honour, that bears the ſtamp of man, and not his nature. You may do what you pleaſe.

Rod. I will do all.

Ped. I do expect thou wilt; for hadſt thou been a noble enemy, thou wouldſt have ſought me whilſt I carried arms, whilſt my good ſword was my profeſſion, and then have cried out, Pedro, I defy thee; then ſtuck Alphonſo's quarrel on thy point. But now, thou poorly, baſely, ſetteſt thy toils to catch me, and like the trembling peaſant, that dares not meet the lion in the face, dig'ſt

dig'ft crafty pit-falls for the generous brute. Thou
fhame to Spanifh honour.

Rod. Thy bravery is to thy habit due: that
holy drefs thou think'ft will be thy fanctuary;
thou wilt not find it fo.

Ped. I look not for't: the more unhallow'd
wretch howe'er art thou t'invade it.

Rod. When you were braveft, fir, and your
fword fharpeft, I durft affront you, you know I
durft; when the court fun gilded you, and every
cry was, The young hopeful Pedro, Alonfo's
fprightly fon ! then I durft meet you, when you
were mafter of this mighty fame, and all your
glories in the full meridian. Had we then come
to competition, which I often fought———

Ped. And I defired too.

Rod. You fhould have feen this fword and felt
it too, fharper than forrow felt it. Then like a
gentleman I would have ufed thee, and given thee
the fair fortune of thy caft: but fince thou fteal'ft
upon me like a fpy, and thief-like think'ft that
holy cafe fhall fave thee, bafe as thy purpofes
thy end fhall be. Soldiers, appear, and bring a
halter with ye. I'll forgive your holy habit, fir,
but I'll hang you.

Enter Lopez, Jaques, *and* Out-Laws.

Jaq. Here's a halter, noble captain: what
fervice have you for't?

Rod. That traytor has fervice for't: trufs him
up.

Jaq. With all my heart: dy'e want a band,
fir? I'll fit it to your collar immediately.

Lop. What's his fault, captain?

Rod. 'Tis my will, he perifh; that's his fault.

Ped. A captain of good government: come,

D 2　　　　　　　　foldiers,

foldiers, come, you are roughly bred, and bloody; fhew your obedience, and the joy you have in executing impious commands. You have a captain feals you liberal pardons: be no more chriftians, 'tis not in your way; put religion by, 'twill make you cowards. Feel no tendernefs; nor let a thing, called confcience, trouble you. Bear no refpect to what I feem; were I a faint indeed, why fhould that ftagger ye? You know no holinefs! to be excellent in evil is your goodnefs; and be fo, 'twill become you; have no hearts, for fear you fhould repent, repentance will be dangerous.

Rod. Trufs up the preacher.

Ped. The racks of confcience are of dire importance; be therefore fteady in your mifchiefs; waver not.

Rod. Up with him, I fay.

Ped. Why do you not obey your chief? Come, this one daring ftroke at heaven will make ye harden'd foldiers of iniquity.

Rod. What do the villains gaze at? Why am I not obey'd?

Jaq. What would you have us do?

Rod. Difpatch the babler——

Jaq. And have religious blood hang o'er our heads? We have fins enough already to make our graves loathe us.

Rod. I fhall not be obey'd then?

Lop. Obey'd? I don't know; though I am a thief, I'm no hangman: they are two trades; I don't care to meddle with holy blood.

Rod. Holy, or unholy, I'll have it done.

Jaq. If I do't I'll be damned.

1ft Out. Or I.

2d Out. Or I. We'll do any thing that's reafonable;

fonable; but the devil would flinch at such a job.

Jaq. I have done as many villanies as another; and, though I fay't, with as few qualms :—— but I don't like this, it goes againſt my ſtomach.

Rod. Have ye then conſpired, ye ſlaves?

Ped Why art thou ſo diſturb'd at their refuſal; if 'tis my life alone thou want'ſt, why with thy own curſt hand doſt thou not take it? Thine's the revenge; be thine the glory.

Rod. 'Tis enough; I'll make ye all repent this ſtubbornneſs; nor will I yet be baffled. Let him not 'ſape, I charge ye, on your lives. [*Exit Rod.*

Jaq. What the devil have you done, pilgrim, to make him rave and rage thus? Have you kill'd his father, or his mother, or ſtrangled any of his kindred?

Lop. Or has he no ſiſters? Han't you been buſy about them?

Jaq. O' my conſcience his quarrel to thee is not for being holier than he.

Lop. Nor for ſeeming an honeſter man; for we have no trading here with ſuch ſtuff. To be excellent thieves is all we aim at. Hark thee, pilgrim, wilt thou take a ſpit and ſtride, and try if thou canſt out-run us?

Ped. No, I ſcorn to ſhift his fury.

Jaq. Thou wilt be hang'd then.

Ped. I cannot die with fewer faults about me.

Jaq. I fancy he'll ſhoot him; for the devil's in't if he hang him himſelf.

Lop. No, he's too proud for that; he'll make ſomebody do't: ſee here he comes again, and as full of rage as ever.

Jaq. He has got the boy with him; ſure he won't make him do't.

Lop. As like as not.   *Enter*

Enter Roderigo *and* Alinda.

Rod. Come, firrah, no wonders. Nay, don't
ftare, nor hang back ; do't, or I'll hang you, you
young dog.

Alin. Alas, fir, what would you have me do ?
Heaven's goodnefs fhield me.

Rod. Do ? Why hang a rogue that would hang
me.

Alin. I'm a boy, and weak, fir ; pray excufe
me.

Rod. Thou art ftrong enough to tie him to a
bough, and turn him off. Come, be quick.

Alin. For heaven's fake, fir.

Rod. Do you difpute, firrah ?

Alin. O, no, fir, I'll do the beft I can. Which
is the man, fir ?

Rod. That in the pilgrim's coat there ; that devil in the faint's fkin.

Alin. Guard me, ye powers.

Rod. Come, difpatch.

Ped. I wait thy worft.

Jaq. to Lop. Will the boy do it ? Is the rogue
fo bold ?

Lop. He fhakes and trembles.

Ped. Doft thou feek more coals ftill to fear thy
confcience ? Work facred innocence to be a devil ? Do it thyfelf, for fhame : Thou beft be-
comeft it.

Rod. Thou art not worthy on't. No, this child
fhall ftrangle thee. A crying girl, if fhe were here,
fhould mafter thee:

Alin. How fhall I fave him ? How myfelf from
violence ? *(afide)* Are you prepared to die, fir ?

Ped. Yes, boy : Prithee to thy bufinefs.

Jaq. The young dog begins to look as if he
would do't in earneft.

Alin.

Alin. If y'are prepared, how can you be fo angry, fo perplexed ? Heaven's won by patience, not by heat and paffion.

Lop. The baftard will make a good prieft.

Ped. I thank thee, gentle child, thou teacheft rightly.

Alin. Methinks you feem to fear too.

Ped. Thou fee'ft more than I feel, boy.

Alin. You tremble fure.

Ped. No, boy, 'tis but thy tendernefs ; prithee make hafte.

. *Alin.* Are you fo willing then to go ?

Ped. Moft willing. I would not borrow from his bounty one poor hour of life, to gain an age of glory.

Alin. And is your reckoning flated right with heaven ?

Ped. As right as truth, boy ; I could not go more joyful to a wedding.

Alin. Then to your prayers ! I'll difpatch you prefently.

Rod. A good boy ; I'll reward thee well.

Alin. I thank you, fir ; but pray allow me a fhort word in private. (*Roderigo figns to Outlaws who retire with Pedro.*)
Now guide my tongue, ye blefled faints above.
(*afide*)

Rod. What wouldft thou have, child ?

Alin. Muft this man die ?

Rod. Why doft thou afk that queftion ?

Alin. Pray be not angry ; if he muft, I'll do it : But muft he now ?

Rod. What elfe : Who dare reprieve him ?

Alin. Pray think again ; and as the injuries are great this man has done you, fo fuit your vengeance to 'em.

Rod.

Rod. I do : 'tis therefore he muſt die——

Alin. A trifle.

Rod. What is a trifle ?

Alin. Death, if he die now.

Rod. Why, my beſt boy ?

Alin. Is it revenge to faint your enemy ? clap the dove's wings of downy peace upon him, and let him ſoar to heaven : Is this revenge ?

Rod. Yet die he muſt.

Alin Right : Let him die, but not prepared to die. That were the bleſſing of a father on him ; and all who know and love revenge would laugh at you. You ſee, thus fortified, he ſcorns your threats ; deſpiſes all your tortures ; ſmiles to behold your rage ; ſo blind your view, that while you aim his hated ſoul to hell, you ſhoot it up to heaven. Shall he die now ?

Lop. What has the boy done to him ?

Jaq. How thoughtfully he looks !

Alin. Come, ſir, you are wiſe, and have the world's regard ; you are valiant too ; ſee then your valour honour'd. 'Twill be a ſtain to both, indeed it will, to have it ſaid, you have given your fury leave to prey on a poor paſſive wayward pilgrim.

Rod. The boy has ſhaken me : What wouldſt thou have me do ?

Alin. Alas, ſir. do you aſk a child ? But ſince you do, I'll ſay the beſt I know. I'd have you then do bravely, ſcorn him, and let him go. You have made him tremble, now feal his pardon ; and when he appears a ſubject fit for anger, fit for you, his pious armour off, his hopes no higher than your ſword may reach, then ſtrike the noble blow. I hope I have turn'd him. *(aſide)*

Rod. Here ; let the fool go. I ſcorn his life too much to take it from him. But if we meet again——   *Ped:*

Ped. I thank ye, fir.

Rod. No more : Be gone.   [*Exit Pedro.*

Alin. Why this was greatly done, moſt noble. But whither is he gone ! O, ſhall we never meet happy ? *(aſide)*

Rod. Come, boy, thou ſhalt retire with me ; I love thy company : Thou haſt a pleaſing tongue ; come with me, child.

Alin. I'll wait upon ye, ſir.—O! Pedro. *(aſide)*
          [*Exeunt Roderigo and Alinda.*

Lop. The boy has don't ; he has ſaved the pil-grim. A cunning young rogue ; I ſhall love him for't heartily.

Jaq. And ſo ſhall I. But the knave's ſo good, I'm afraid he'll ruin us, he'll make us all honeſt.

1ſt Out. Marry, heaven forbid.

2d Out. He'll find that a harder taſk than to ſave the pilgrim.

Lop. That I believe : But come, gentlemen, let's to ſupper ; we'll drink the boy's health, and ſo about our buſineſs.   [*Exeunt.*

A C T   III.

S C E N E II. *The Foreſt and Cave.*

Enter Roderigo, Jaquez, Lopez, *and Out-laws.*

Rod. 'TIS ſtrange none of you ſhou'd know her.

Jaq. Alas ! we never ſaw her, nor heard of her but from you.

E   *Lop.*

Lop. I don't think 'twas fhe ; methinks a woman fhould not dare ———

Rod. Thou fpeak'ft thou know'ft not what:
What dare not woman when fhe is provoked ?
That it is fhe, thefe jewels here confirm me ; for
part of them I myfelf fent her, which (tho' againft
her will) her father forced her to accept and
wear.

Lop. 'Tis very ftrange, a wench, and we not
know it ; I ufed to have a better nofe.

Jaq. But what could be her bufinefs here ?

Rod. That's what diftracts me. O that cant-
ing pilgrim, that villain Pedro ! There lies my
torture, How cunningly fhe pleaded for him !
How artfully fhe faved him ! Death and tor-
ments, had ye been true to me, I ne'er had fuf-
fer'd this.

Jaq. Why you might have hang'd him if you
would ; and would he had been hang'd, that's all
we care for't, fo we had not don't———

Rod. But where is fhe now ? What care have
ye had of that ? Why have ye let her go, to def-
pife and laugh at me ?

Lop. The devil that brought her hither, has
carried her back again, I think ; for none of
us faw her go.

Jaq. No living thing came this night through
our watches. You know fhe went with you.

Rod. And was by me, till I fell afleep : But,
when I waked and call'd, was gone. Curfe on
my dulnefs, why did I not open this ? This
would have told me all.

Enter Alphonfo *and Outlaws.*

Alph. Prithee bring me to thy captain, where's
thy captain, fellow ? Oh, I am founder'd, I am
melted ;

melted ; the devil has enticed me with the voice of a wench. Where's thy captain, fellow ?

1st Out. Here, sir, there he stands.

Alph. O captain, how dost thou, captain ? I have been fool'd, bubbled, made an afs on : My daughter's run away ; I have been haunted too ; have lost my horse, am starved for want of meat, and out of my wits.

Rod. I'm sorry, sir, to see you engaged in so many misfortunes : But pray walk in, refresh yourself, and I'll inform you what has happen'd here ; but I'll recover your daughter, or lose my life.

Alph. My daughter be damn'd. Order me drink enough ; I'm almost choak'd.

Rod. You shall have any thing. [*Exit Alph.* What think you now, soldiers ?

Jaq. I think, a woman's a woman ; that's all. [*Exit Rod.*

Lop. And I think the next boy we take, we should search him a little nearer. [*Exeunt.*

Enter Juletta.

Jul. This is Roderigo's quarter ; my old master's gone in here, and I'll be with him soon; I'll startle him a little better than I have done. All this long night have I led him out of the way, to try his patience. I have made him swear and curse, and pray and curse again : I have made him lose his horse too, whistled him through thick and thin. Down in a ditch I had him ; there he lay bellowing, till I call'd him out to guide his nose pop into a furz-bush. Ten thousand tricks I have play'd him, and ten thousand will add to them, before I have done with him. I'll teach him to

plague

plague poor young woman. But all this while
I can't meet with my dear miſtreſs. I'm cruelly
afraid ſhe ſhould be in diſtreſs; would I could
come to comfort her: But, till I do, I'll haunt
thy ghoſt, Alphonſo; I will, old crab-tree. He
ſhan't ſleep; I'll get a drum for him, I'll frighten
him out of his wits; I have ſuch a hurricane in
my head, I have almoſt loſt my own already;
and I'm reſolved I won't be mad alone. When
a woman ſets upon playing the devil, 'twere a
ſhame ſhe ſhould not do't to the purpoſe. [*Exit.*

S C E N E II. *Another Part of the Foreſt.*

Enter Seberto *and* Curio.

Seb. 'Tis ſtrange, in all the tour we have made,
we ſhould have no news at all of her.

Cur. I can't think ſhe's got ſo far.

Seb. She's certainly diſguiſed; her modeſty
would never venture in her own ſhape.

Cur. Let her take any ſhape, I'm ſure I could
diſtinguiſh her.

Seb. So could I, I think. Has not her father
found her?

Cur. Not he, he's ſo wild he would not know
her, if he met her.

Seb. I hope he would not; for 'tis pity ſhe
ſhould fall into his hands. But where are we,
Curio?

Cur. In a wood, I think; hang me if I know
elſe: And yet I have ridden all theſe coaſts, and
at all hours.

Seb. I wiſh we had a guide.

Cur. If I am not much miſtaken, Seberto, we
are not far from Roderigo's quarters. I think it
is in this thicket he and his Outlaws harbour.

Seb.

Seb. Then we are where Alphonfo appointed to meet us.

Cur. I believe we are; would we could meet fome living thing to inform us.

Seb. What's that there ?

Cur. A boy, I think; ftay, why may not he di-rect us ?

Enter Alinda.

Alin. I am hungry, and I am weary, almoft fpent, yet çannot find him ; keep me in my wits, good heaven ! O my head.

. *Seb.* Hey, boy, doft hear, thou ftripling ?

Alin. O my fears, fome of Roderigo's wicked crew. If I am carried back to him, I then indeed am wretched.

Cur. Doft know what place this is, child ?

Alin. No, indeed, fir, not I.   O my bones !

Seb. What doft thou complain for, boy ? A very pretty lad this.

Cur. What's the matter with thee, child ?

Alin. Alas, fir, I was going to Segovia, to fee my fick mother, and here I have been taken, robb'd, and beaten by drunken thieves.   O my head !

Seb. What rogues are thefe to ufe a poor boy thus ! look up, child, be of good cheer, hold up thy head.

Alin. O I cannot, it hurts me if I do ; they have given me a great blow on the neck.

Cur. What thieves are they, doft know ?

Alin. They call the captain Roderigo. O dear, O dear.

Cur. Look you there ; I knew we were there-abouts.

Seb. Doft thou want any thing ?

Alin.

Alin. Nothing but cafe, fir.

Cur. There's fome money for thee, however, and get thee to thy mother.

Alin. I thank ye, gentlemen; pray heaven blefs ye.

Seb. Come, let's along, we can't lofe our way now.   [*Exeunt Seberto and Curio.*

Alin. I'm glad you are gone, gentlemen; I know you are honeft men, but I don't know whether you are on my fide upon this occafion : Lord, how I tremble, fend me but once into Pedro's arms, dear fortune, and then come what will——— Which way fhall I go, or what fhall I do? 'tis almoft night again, and I know not where to get either meat or lodging. Thefe wild woods, and the various fancies that poffefs my brain, will run me mad. Hey ho !

Enter Juletta *with a drum.*

Jul. Boy ! boy !

Alin. More fet to take me.

Jul. Doft hear, boy ? A word with thee.

Alin. 'Tis a boy too, I can deal with him.

Jul. Hark ye, young man; can you beat a drum ?

Alin. A drum !

Jul. A drum ! ay, a drum; didft never fee a drum, man ? Prithee try if thou canft make it grumble.

Alin. (*afide.*) Juletta's face and tongue; is fhe run mad too? Or is there fome defign in this? I'm jealous of every thing

Jul. I'll give thee a ryal, but to go along with me to-night, and hurry durry this a little.

Alin. I care not for your ryal nor you neither,
                                                    I have

I have other bufinefs; prithee drum to thyfelf
and dance to't.

Jul. Why, how now, you faucy young dog
you! I have a good mind to lay down my drum,
and take ye a flap o'er the face.

Alin. Hark, here comes more company, I fhall
be taken at laft. Heaven fhield me!   [*Exit.*

Jul. Bafto! who's there?

    Enter Roderigo, Lopez, *and Outlaws.*

Lop. Do you need me any farther, captain?

Rod. No, not a foot: give me the fword.

Jul. This is the devil thief; and, if he take me,
woe be to my little gafkins. (*afide*)

Lop. Certainly, fir, fhe'll change her habit.

Rod. Let her do what fhe will, fhe can't again
deceive me. No, no, Alinda, 'tis not the habit
of a boy can twice delude me.

Jul. A boy. what a dull jade have I been! (*afide.*

Rod. If fhe be found i'th' woods, fend me word
prefently, and I'll return; fhe can't be got far.
If you don't find her, expect me —— when you
fee me. No more; farewel.

    [*Exeunt Rod. and Outlaws feparately.*

Jul. I'm very glad thou art gone. This boy
was the boy I talk'd to: the very fame, how
haftily it fhifted me! what a mop-ey'd afs was I,
I could not know her. It muft be fhe; 'tis fhe:
now I remember, how loath fhe was to talk; how
fhy fhe was of me. I'll follow her; but who fhall
plague her father there? No, I muft not quit him
yet: I muft have one flirt more at him, and then
for the voyage. Come, drum, make ready. Thou
muft do me fervice.   [*Exit.*

                SCENE

S C E N E III. *The Foreſt and Cave.*

Enter Jaquez *and Outlaws.*

Jaq. Are they all ſet?

1ſt Out. All, and each quarter's quiet.

Jaq. Is old Alphonſo aſleep?

1ſt Out. An hour ago.

Jaq. We muſt be very careful in our captain's abſence.

1ſt Out. It concerns us, he won't be long from us—— (*drum beats.*) Hark!——

Jaq. What!

1ſt Out. A drum.

Jaq. The devil!

1ſt Out. 'Tis not the wind, ſure.

Jaq. No, that's ſtill and calm—(*drum again.*) Hark, again.

1ſt Out. Tat, tat.

Jaq. It comes nearer: we are ſurprized; 'tis by the King's command; we are all dead men.

(*A charge by drum.*

1ſt Out. Hark, hark, a charge now. Our captain has betray'd us all.

Jaq. This comes of love. Poverty, a ſcolding wife, and ten daughters be his recompence.

Enter Lopez, *and Outlaws.*

Lop. D'ye hear the drum?

Jaq. Yes, we do hear it. (*Drum again.*

1ſt Out. Hark, another on that ſide.

Enter third Outlaw.

3d Out. Fly, fly, fly! we are all taken, we are all taken! A thouſand horſe and foot, a thouſand pioneers and every man a halter by his ſide.

Lop.

Lop. A difmal night, companions! what's to be done?

Jaq. Every man fhift for himfelf. (*drum again.*
[*Exeunt feverally.*

Enter Alphonfo, *and an Outlaw.*

Alph. Ay, marry, fir, where's my horfe now? What a plague did I do amongft thefe rogues? Is there ne'er a hole to creep into? I fhall be taken for their captain, and out of refpect to my poft, be hang'd up firft. A plague of all cere-monies, cry I : what will become of me? I muft be a daughter-hunting, with a plague to me: Lord! Lord! that a foolifh young jade fhould lead a wife old rogue into fo much mifchief. But hark; hark, I fay : ay, here they come. That I had but the ftrumpet here now, to find 'em a little play while I made my efcape——

Enter Seberto, Curio, *and Outlaws.*

Seb. What do you fear? What do you run from? Here are no foldiers, nobody from the King to attack you : are you all mad?

Lop. Ay, but the drum; the drum, fir, did not you hear the drum?

Cur. I never faw fuch pigeon-hearted rogues; what drum, you fools? What danger? Who's that ftands fhaking there behind, enough to infect a whole army with cowardice. Mercy on me, fir, is't you? What is't that frights you thus?

Alph. Are there any hopes; do ye think I could buy my pardon?

Seb. What is't that has frighted you thus out of your fenfes? Here's no danger near you : a drum I heard indeed, and faw it, a boy was beat-ing it; hunting fquirrels by moon-light.

Cur. Nothing elfe, upon my word, fir,

F   *Alph.*

Alph. That rogue, the very boy, no doubt on't, that haunted me all laft night. I wifh I had him, he has plagued my heart out. But come, let's go in, and let me get on my cloaths; if I ftay here any longer to be martyr'd thus, I'll beget another daughter. Where is that jewel? Have you met her yet?

Seb. No; we have no news of her.

Alph. Then I can tell you fome; fhe has been here in boy's cloaths, fhe has trufs'd up her o-defly in a pair of breeches. There has been a pilgrim with her too. I fuppofe the game's al-moft up by this time.

Cur. A young boy we met, fir.

Alph. Dreft in blue?

Cur. Dreft in blue.

Alph. The ftrumpet.

Cur. Impoffible!

Alph. True——in the literal fenfe.

Seb. 'Tis wonderful we fhould not know her.

Alph. Damn her; that's all. Come, get me fome wine, a great deal: this halter makes me keckle in the throat ftill.   [*Exeunt.*

S C E N E IV. *A Chamber in a Mad-houfe.*

Enter Keepers.

1ft Keep. Carry mad Befs fome meat, fhe roars like thunder. And tie the parfon fhort. Who looks to the 'prentice? Keep him from women; 'twill run him horn-mad.

2d Keep. The juftice keeps fuch a ftir yonder with his charges, and fuch a coil with his warrants.

1ft Keep. Take away his ftatutes; the devil has poffefs'd him in the likenefs of penal laws. How is't with the fcholar?

                                        2d Keep.

2d Keep. For any thing I see he is in's right wits.

1ſt Keep. Thou art an aſs; his head's too full of other people's wits, to leave room for his own. But come, let's away and ſerve 'em.   [*Exeunt*

S C E N E V. *Cells in the Mad-houſe.*

Enter Keepers, and mad Engliſhman.

Engl. Give me ſome drink.

1ſt Keep. O ho! here's the Engliſhman.

Engl. Fill me a thouſand pots, and froth 'em, froth 'em; down o'your knees, you rogues, and pledge me roundly; one, two, three——and four. To the great Turk, I'm his friend, and will pre-fer him; he ſhall quit his crown———and be a tapſter.

1ſt Keep. Peace, thou heatheniſh drunkard, peace for ſhame. Theſe Engliſh are malt-mad; when they have a fruitful year of barley, the whole iſland's thus.

Engl. Who talks of barley? My drink's ſmall; down with the malt-tax Huzza. Who's that? An exciſeman? The devil.

Enter a She-Fool.

Fool. Give you a good even, gaffer. Will ye walk into the coal-houſe, gaffer?

1ſt Keep. Who a vengeance looks to her? Go in, Kate, go in, and I'll give thee a fine apple.

Fool. Will you buſs me, and play with me, and make me laugh.

1ſt Keep. I'll ſcourge you, huſſy.

Engl. Fool, fool, come to me, fool.

Fool. And ſhall I have a coach?

Engl. Drawn with four turkies.

Fool. Turkies! O dear me! we ſhall have eggs then.

Engl. Ay, ay, and they fhall be all addle, and make a tanzy for the devil. Come, come away, fool.

1ft Keep. Here comes my mafter. Away with 'em both. [*Exeunt Keep. with the madman and fool.*

Enter *Mafter, two Gentlemen and Mad Scholar.*

1ft Gent. I'll affure you, fir, the cardinal's angry with you for keeping this young man.

Maft. I'm heartily forry, fir: If you allow him found, pray take him with you.

2d Gent. We can find nothing in him light nor tainted ; no ftarts, no rubs in all his anfwers : His letters too are full of difcretion, learning, and in a handfome ftile.

Maft. Don't be deceived, fir ; mark but his look.

1ft Gent. His grief and his imprifonment may ftamp that there.

Maft. Pray talk with him again then.

2d Gent. That will be needlefs, we hawe tried him long enough ; and if he had a taint, we fhould have met with't. You find no ficknefs ?

Scho. None, fir, I thank heaven ; nor nothing that difturbs my underftanding.

1ft Gent. Do you fleep a nights ?

Scho. Perfectly found and fweet.

2d. Gent. Have you no fearful dreams ?

Scho. Sometimes, as all have who go to bed with raw and windy ftomachs.

1ft Gent. Is there no unkindnefs you have received from any friend, or parent ? or fcorn from what you loved ?

Scho. No, truly fir, I have not yet feen villainy enough to make me doubt the truth of friend

or

or kindred—and what love is, unlefs it lie in learning, I am ignorant.

1ſt Gent. This man is perfect; I never met with one that talk'd more regularly.

Maſt. You'll find it otherwife.

2d Gent. I muſt tell you plainly, fir, I think you keep him here to make him mad; but here's his difcharge from my lord cardinal. Come, fir, you are now at liberty to go with us.

Scho. I thank ye, gentlemen : Maſter, farewel.

Maſt. Farewel, Stephano. Alas! poor man.

1ſt Gent. What flaws and guſts of weather we have had thefe three days ! How dark and hot it is ! The ſky is full of mutiny.

2d Gent. Strange work at fea, I doubt.

1ſt Gent. Blefs my old uncle's bark, I have a venture in't.

2d Gent. And fo have I, more than I'd wiſh to lofe ; I'm in fome fear.

Scho. Do you fear ?

2d Gent. Mercy on me, how he ſtares !

Maſt. Now tell me how ye like him ? What think ye of him for a fober man now ?

Scho. Does the fea ſtagger ye ? Do ye fear the billows ?

1ſt Gent. What ails him ? who has ſtirr'd him ?

Scho. Be not ſhaken : Let the ſtorm rife ; let it blow on, blow on : Let the clouds wreſtle, and let the vapours of the earth turn mutinous. The fea in hideous mountains rife, and tumble upon a dolphin's back ; I'll make all ſhake, for I am Neptune.

Maſt. Now, what think you of him ?

2d Gent. Alas, poor man !

Scho. Your bark ſhall plough through all, and

not

not a furge fo faucy to difturb her : I'll fee her
fafe ; my power fhall fail before her——
    Down, ye angry waters all,
    Ye loud whiftling whirlwinds, fall.
    Down, ye proud waves ; ye ftorms, ceafe,
    I command ye be at peace ;
    Fright not with your churlifh notes,
    Nor bruife the keel of bark that floats.
    No devouring fifh come nigh,
    Nor Monfter, in my empery ;
    Once fhew his head, or terror bring ;
    But let the weary failor fing.
    Amphitrite, with white arms,
    Strike my lute ; I'll fing charms.

Maft. Now he muft have mufic ; then he'll
go in quietly of himfelf, and clean forget all.
(*Soft mufic*)   [*Exeunt feverally.*

End of Act III.

A C T   IV.

S C E N E I. *The Country near* Sogovia.

Enter Alphonfo, *and a Gentleman.*

Juletta *follows 'em unfeen.*

Gen. YOU are now within a mile o'th' town,
    fir ; if my bufinefs would give me
leave, I'd guide ye farther. But for fuch gentlemen as you enquire for, I have feen none.
                           The

The boy you defcribe, or one much like it, was fent in t'other night a little maddifh, and now is in the houfe appointed for fuch cures,

Alph. 'Tis very well, I thank ye, fir.

Jul. (*afide*) And fo do I : for if there be fuch a place, I afk no more. You fhall hear of me, i'faith, old gentleman ; I'll follow you there too, as tired as I am ; and make ye kick and roar before I have done with you. I'll teach you to haunt mad-houfes.

Alph. (*afide*) It muft be fhe. 'Tis very well : Is your blood fo hot, i'faith, my minx ? I'll have ye madded, I'll have ye worm'd.

Gent. Here's one belongs to the very houfe, fir; 'tis a poor ideot, but fhe'll fhew you the way as well as a wifer body. So, fir, I leave you.

Alph. Your fervant. [*Exit Gent.*
Here, fool, a word with thee, fool.

Enter Alinda, *as the She-fool.*

Alin. O, I am loft ! 'Tis my father in all his rage. (*afide*)

Alph. Hark thee, fool.

Alin. He does not know me ; heaven grant I may deceive him ftill ! (*afide*) Will ye give me two-pence, gaffer, and here's a crow-flower, and a daify; I have fome pye in my pocket too.

Alph. This is an arrant fool, a meer changeling.

Alin. Think fo, and I am happy. (*afide*)

Alph. Doft thou dwell in Segovia, fool ?

Alin. No, no, I dwell in heaven ; and I have a fine houfe made of marmalade ; and I am a lone woman, and I fpin for St. Peter. I have a hundred little children, and they fing pfalms with me.

Alph.

Alph. A very pretty converſation I am falling into here, eſpecially for a man in a paſſion. Canſt thou tell me if this be the way to the town?

Alin. Yes, yes, you muſt go over the top of that high ſteeple, gaffer.

Alph. A plague of your fool's face.

Jul. (*aſide*) No; take her counſel, do.

Alin. And then you ſhall come to a river, gaffer, twenty miles over, and twenty miles and ten; and then you muſt pray, gaffer, and pray, and pray, and pray, and pray, and pray.

Alph. Pray heaven deliver me from ſuch an aſs as thou art.

Alin. Amen, ſweet gaffer; and then you muſt leap in naked.

Jul. (*aſide.*) Would to heav'n he would take her counſel.

Alin. And ſink ſeven days together. Can ye ſink, gaffer?

Alph. Plague on thee, and a plague o'that fool that left me to thee.   [*Exit Alph.*

Alin. God be w'ye, nuncle.

Jul. How I rejoice in any thing that vexes him! I ſhall love this fool as long as I live, for putting her hand to the plough. Could I but ſee my miſtreſs now, to tell her how I have labour'd for her; how I have worn myſelf away in her ſervice; —Well, ſure, I ſhall find her at laſt.

Alin. (*aſide.*) 'Tis Juletta.—Sure ſhe's honeſt; yet I dare not diſcover myſelf to her.

Jul. Here, fool, here's ſomething for thee to buy apples, for the ſport thou haſt made in croſſing thy nuncle.

Alin. Thank ye, little gentleman; pray keep this nutmeg; 'twas ſent me from the lady of the mountain, a golden lady.

Jul.

Jul. How prettily it prattles!

Alin. 'Tis very good to rub your underſtanding; and ſo good night; the moon's up.

Jul. Pretty innocence!

Alin. (*aſide.*) Now, fortune, if thou dareſt do good, protect me. [*Exit Alinda.*

Jul. I'll follow him to the town; he ſhan't eſcape me.—Let me ſee—I muſt counterfeit a letter, a letter of authority for him——Yes, 'twill do; certainly do. How I ſhall make his old blood boil! rare ſport, i'faith! but what i'th' name of innocence has this fool given me? ſhe ſaid 'twas good to rub my underſtanding.—Hah! a ring! a right one! a ring I know too!——The very ſame——A ring my miſtreſs took from me, and wore it: I know it by the poeſy. None could deliver this but ſhe herſelf. 'Twas ſhe. Curſe o'my ſand-blind eyes. Twice deceived! twice ſo near the bleſſing I am ſeeking! what ſhall I do? Here are ſo many croſs ways, 'tis in vain to follow her. I hope, however, for all her dreſs, ſhe's in her ſenſes ſtill, for ſure ſhe knew me.——Well, to divert my melancholy, 'till I can meet her again, I'll e'en go and plague the old fellow a little more.

[*Exit Juletta.*

SCENE II. *A Wood.*

Enter Roderigo.

Rod. She's not to be recover'd; and, which doubles my torment, he's got beyond my vengeance. How they laugh at me!——Look to't, my young deceiver; we ſhall meet, which when we do, not all the tears and cries of trembling chaſtity ſhall ſave thee.

G   *Enter*

Enter Alinda.

Alin. Is not that Pedro ? 'Tis he ; 'tis he: ——
Oh my ———

Rod. What art thou ?

Alin. Hah !——Oh ! I'm miserable.   (*aside.*

Rod. What the devil art thou ?

Alin. (*aside.*) No end of my misfortunes ? Hea-
v'ns ! that habit to betray me ! ye holy powers, can
ye see that ? Do yourselves justice, and protect me.

Rod. Hey-day ! the devil in a fool's coat ! Is
he turn'd changling ? Is't not a fairy ? It has a
mortal face. But if it should prove the devil !——

Alin. Come hither, dear.

Rod. It's a handsome thing. What's that it
points at ?

Alin. Dost thou see that star there ? That just
above the sun ? Prithee go thither, and light me
this tobacco, and stop it with the horns of the
moon.

Rod. The Thing's mad, quite mad. Go sleep,
fool, go sleep.

Alin. Thou canst not sleep so quietly ; for I can
say my prayers, and then slumber.

     I am not proud, nor full of wine ;
     This little flow'r will make me fine :
     Cruel in heart, for I will cry
     If I see a sparrow die.
     I am not watchful to do ill,
     Nor glorious to pursue it still ;
     Nor pitiless to those that weep,
     Such as are, bid them go sleep.
Do, do, do ; and see if they can.

Rod. It said true. Its words sink into me.
                            Sure

Sure 'tis a kind of fybil; fome mad prophet. I
feel my fury bound and fetter'd in me.

Alin. Give me your hand, and I'll tell you your
fortune.

Rod. Here, prithee do.

Alin. Fie ! fie ! fie ! fie ! fie ! Wafh your
hands and pare your nails, and look finely, you
fhall never kifs the king's daughter elfe.

Rod. I wafh 'em daily.

Alin. But foul 'em fafter.

Rod. (*afide*) This goes nearer me.

Alin. You fhall have two wives.

Rod. Two wives !

Alin. Yes; two fine gentlewomen. Make
much of 'em, for they'll ftick clofe to you, fir.
And thefe two in two days, fir.

Rod. That's a fine riddle !

Alin. To-day you fhall wed forrow, and repentance will come to-morrow.

Rod. Sure fhe's infpired.

Alin. I'll bid you a good even; for my boat
ftays for me, and I muft fup with the moon to-
night in the Mediterranean.   [*Exit Alinda.*

Rod. Can fools and mad-folks then be tutors
to me ? Can they feel my fores, yet I infenfible ?
Sure this was fent by providence to fteer me right.
I'm wondrous weary; my thoughts too, they are
tired, which adds a weighty burden to me. I have
done ill; I have purfued it too; nay, ftill run on.
I muft think better; be fomething elfe or nothing.
Still I grow heavier. A little reft would help
me; I'll try if I can take it; and heaven's goodnefs guard me.   [*Lies down.*

Enter

Enter several Peasants.

1*st Pea.* We have 'scaped to-day well. If the Outlaws had known we had been stirring, we had paid for't, neighbours.

2*d Pea.* A murrain take 'em, they have robb'd me thrice.

3*d Pea.* Me five times, my daughter fifty ; tho', to give them their due, they ne'er take any thing from her, but what she can very well spare.

2*d Pea.* Ah ! my poor wife has been in their hands too : but, to say the truth, I don't find she has lost much neither.

1*st Pea.* For my part, I ought not to complain, for I have got three children by 'em.

2*d Pea.* Would we had some of 'em here, to thank 'em, for their kindnesses.

3*d Pea.* So we were strong enough, I don't care if we had.

2*d Pea.* What's that lies there ?

1*st Pea.* An old woman that keeps sheep hereabouts.

3*d Pea.* And a sword by her side to keep the wolves off?——Hah ! captain Roderigo, or the devil.——Stand to your arms, gentlemen, 'tis he.

1*st Pea.* Speak softly.

2*d Pea.* Now's our time.

3*d Pea.* Stay, stay, let's be provident, Shall we wake him before we kill him, or after ?

2*d Pea.* Let me kill my share of him before he wakes.

1*st Pea.* Let me have the first blow ; he robb'd me last.

2*d Pea.* No, I ought to have the first ; he cuckolded me last.

3*d Pea.* Hold, hold ; no civil wars, d'ye hear ?

Beat

Beat his brains out between ye——And then I'll pick his pockets.   (*aſide.*)

2d Pea. Draw your knives, and every man ſeize a limb.

Omn. Huzza !

Rod. Slaves ! villains ! will ye murder me ?

1ſt Pea. No, no ; we'll only tickle you a little. D'ye remember Joan, captain ? I'll ſpoil ye for a cuckold-maker.

Rod. For heaven's ſake ! as ye are men; as y'are chriſtians.

1ſt Pea. Neither man nor chriſtian, upon this occaſion; but a cuckold with my knife in my hand.

Rod. Murder ! murder !

Enter Pedro.

Ped. Off, ye inhuman ſlaves !——Nay, then have among ye.

Omn. Away, away, away.   [*Exeunt Peaſants.*

Ped. Villains ! uſe violence to that habit !

Rod. Pedro !——Nay, then I am more wretch-ed than ever.   (*aſide.*)

Ped. Hah ! Roderigo !—What makes him here thus clad ? Is it repentance, or a diſguiſe for miſ-chief ?   (*aſide.*)

Rod. To owe my life to him makes me all con-fuſion.   (*aſide.*)

Ped. You are not much hurt, ſir ?

Rod. No.——All, I can call a wound, is in my conſcience.   (*aſide.*)

Ped. Have ye conſider'd the nature of theſe men, and how they have uſed you ? Was it well?

Rod. (*aſide.*) I cannot ſpeak, for I have nought to anſwer.

Ped.

Ped. Lid it look noble to be o'erlaid with odds?
Did it seem manly in a multitude to opprefs you?
If it be bafe in wretches low like thefe, what muft
it be in one that's born like you? Ah, Roderigo!
had I abandon'd honefty, religion, broke through
the bonds of honour and humanity, I had fet as
fmall a price upon thy life, as thou didft lately
upon mine : but I referve thee to a nobler vengeance.

Rod. I thank ye ; you have the nobler foul, I
muft confefs it ; and of your paffions are a greater
mafter. Th' example's glorious, and I wifh to
follow it. There is a ftain of infamy about me,
and the dye is deep ; yet poffibly occafion may
prefent, that I may wafh it off.

Ped. I'll give you one, a noble one, I think.
We have a quarrel, we've a miftrefs too. We
are fingle, and our arms alike. In one fair rifque
of life let all determine, our rancour paft, and
happinefs to come.

Rod. (*afide.*) His virtue ftaggers me.——I dare
fight, Pedro.

Ped. I do believe you dare : cr, if you wanted
courage, the beauteous prize, for which we now
contend, would rouze you to't.

Rod. Hah !

Ped. If you deferve her, draw.

Rod. I do not, nor fuch a noble enemy : I
therefore will not draw.

Ped. I could compel you to't, but would not
willingly.

Rod. You cannot, to increafe my guilt : the
load's already more than I can bear; I wo'not
add to't.

Ped. Poor evafion.

Rod.

Rod. Thou wrong'ft me ; much thou wrong'ft me, time will convince thee on't. I'll fatisfy thee any way but this. I have been wicked, but cannot be a monfter. My fword refufes to attempt the man preferv'd me. Its temper ftarts at thy virtue. If thou wilt have me fight give me an enemy, for thou art none.

Ped. I'm more ; for I'm thy rival.

Rod. That is not in thy power : for I no more am thine. No, Pedro ; the wrongs I've done myfelf and thee, let that fair faint atone for : there's nothing more I or the world can give ; and nothing lefs can expiate my crimes, or recompence thy virtue.

Ped. Is't poffible thou canft be fuch a penitent !

Rod. I am moft truly fuch ; and left I fhould relapfe again to hell, forget the debt I owe to thee and heav'n ; this facred habit, I have fo profaned, fhall henceforth be my faithful monitor.

Ped. Noble Roderigo, how glorious is this change ! Let me embrace thee.

Rod. Thou great example of humanity, doft thou forgive me ?

Ped. I do ; with joy I do.

Rod. Then I am happy.—All I have more to afk, is, leave to attend you in your prefent difficulties ; that, by fuch fervice as I have power to render, I may confirm you, I am what I feem.

Ped. There needs no further proof : however, in hopes I doubly may return thofe fervices, I'll not refufe 'em.   [*Exeunt.*

SCENE

SCENE III. *A Chamber in the Mad-houſe.*

Enter Alphonſo *and Maſter.*

Maſt. Yes, ſir, here are ſuch people : but how pleaſing they may be to you, I can't tell.

Alph. That's not your concern ; I deſire to ſee 'em, to ſee 'em all.

Maſt. All ? They are nothing but confuſion, meer noiſe.

Alph. May be I love noiſe ?——But hark ye, ſir ; have ye no boys, handſome young boys ?

Maſt. One, ſir, we have; a very handſome boy.

Alph. Long here ?

Maſt. But two days : A little crazed, but may recover.

Alph. That boy, I would ſee that boy ; per-haps I know him.——(*aſide*) This is the boy he told me of ; it muſt be ſhe——The boy, maſter, I beſeech ye, the boy.

Maſt. Well, well, ſir, have a little patience, come with me and you ſhall ſee him.

Alph. Ay, ay, the boy ! the boy !　　[*Exeunt.*

SCENE IV. *Cells in the Mad-houſe.*

Enter Keepers, and She-Fool in Alinda's *Clothes, meeting* Alphonſo *and Maſter.*

1ſt *Keep.* Huſſy ! who did this for you ?

Maſt. Where's the boy, you ſlut you ? where's the boy ?

Fool. The boy's gone a maying ; he'll bring me home a cuckoo's neſt. He gave me theſe trim clothes too, and put 'em on he did.

Alph.

Alph. Is this the boy you'd fhew me ?

Fool. I'll give you two-pence, mafter.

Alph. Am I fool'd on all fides ? I met a fool in the wood in a long pied coat; they faid fhe dwelt here.

Maft. That was the very boy, fir.

Fool. Ay, ay, ay ; I gave him leave to play, forfooth ; he'll come again to-morrow. . [*Retires.*

Alph. Plague o'your fools and bedlams ; plague o'your owls and apes.

Maft. Pray, fir, be moderate ; fuch accidents will happen fometimes, take what care we can.

Alph. Damn accidents! You're a juggler, and I'm abufed.

Maft. Indeed, fir, you are not.

Alph. It's falfe ; I am abufed, and I will be abufed, whether you will or no, fir. Who lies here ?

1ft Keep. Pray don't difturb 'em, fir ; there lie fuch youths will make you ftart, if they begin to dance.

Maft. Hark!

Alph. Hey boys !

Enter Englifh *Madman.*

Engl. Bounce : clap her o'th' ftarboard. Bounce : top the can. Bounce : 'twixt wind and water : laden with Mackerel !—Oh brave meat !

Alph. Brave fport, i'faith !

Engl. I'll drink up all. Bounce I fay once more—O ho ! have I fplit your mizen ? Blow, blow, thou weft-wind ; blow till thou rife, and make the fea run roaring ;—I'll hifs it down again, with a bottle of ale.

H   *Alph.*

Alph. Mad gallants, mad gallants, i'faith; I love their fancies, I never fell into better company in my life.

Enter mad Taylor.

Tay. Who's that ?——The King of Spades ? I'll make him a new mantle.

Alph. Hey day : a mad taylor too ! What the pox made thee mad ?

Tay. Cabbage——Snip goes the fheers—and the coat's never the fhorter.

Alph. Thou'rt a brave fellow, and fha't make me a new doublet.

Tay. For thy coronation—I'll do't ; but money down ; doft hear ? money down. The King of Spades is a courtier—Money down—ay, and cabbage too.

Alph. Well, well, thou fhalt have cabbage and beef too.   [*Exit Taylor.*

Engl. Who talks of beef ?—'tis mine by Magna Charta—Beef ! ye gods, beef !—I'll have that ox for fupper—knock him down—Chines ! furloins ! ribs ! and rounds !——Lead me to the French camp—— They fly ! they fly ! they fly ! they fly ! huzza !   [*Exit.*

Alph. I'gad I'll fee him in's lodging ; I have a mind to fup with him. He feems as if he'd be rare company over a bottle.   [*Exit.*

Enter Juletta.

Jul. (*afide*) He's in, and now have at him— Ar' you the mafter, fir ?

Maft. Yes. What do you want ?

Jul. I have a bufinefs from the duke of Medina. Is there not an old gentleman come lately here ?

Maft.

Maſt. Yes ; and a mad one too ; but he's no priſoner.

Jul. There's a letter ; pray read it.——(*afide*) I ſhall be with you now, i'faith, my old maſter ; I'll rouſe your blood now to the purpoſe : I'll teach ye to plague poor young women, ye old put you.

Maſt. This letter ſays the getleman is lunatic : I half ſuſpected it.

Jul. 'Tis but too true, ſir : and ſuch pranks he has play'd——

Maſt. The duke's in haſte, I find, for his reco-very ; for he bids me ſpare no correction.

Jul. He directed me to ſay the ſame thing to you. Pray, ſir, have no regard to his age or quality : but ſince 'tis for his good, ſtrap him ſoundly.

Maſt. Pray how did you get him hither ?

Jul. By a train I laid for him ; he's in love with a boy you muſt know ; there lies his crack.

Maſt. He came hither to ſeek one.

Jul. Yes, I ſent him. We ſhould never have got him here by force.

Maſt. Here was a boy laſt night.

Jul. He did not ſee him, did he ?

Maſt. No.

Jul. So much the better. Pray, ſir, look well to your charge : I muſt ſee him lodged be-fore I go ; the Duke order'd me. I fancy you'll find him very rough.

Maſt. We can be as rough as he, I'll warrant him.

Jul. See, here he comes——(*afide*) O how it tickles me !

H 2 *Enter*

Enter Alphonso *and second Keeper.*

Alph. What doft thou talk to me of noifes?
I'll have more noife : I love noife. I'll have 'em
all loofe together. Your mafter has let my boy
loofe, and I'll do as much by his.

2d Keep. Will you go out, and not make dif-
turbances here?

Alph. I won't go out, you rafcal; I'll have 'em
all out with me. There's nobody mad here, but
thee and thy mafter.——(*Irons fhake.*) B'...y, brave
boys! mad boys! mad boys!

Jul. Do you perceive him now?

Maft. Sir, Pray will you make lefs ftir, and
fee your chamber?

Alph. Ha!

Maft. Come, fir, will you retire quietly to your
chamber?

Alph. My chamber! what doft thou mean by
my chamber? Where's the boy, you blockhead
you?

Maft. Look ye, fir, we are people of few words
here; either go quietly to your chamber, or we
fhall carry you there with a witnefs.

Alph. A ftrange fellow this!——And what chamber is't thou wouldft have me go quietly to?

Maft. A chamber the Duke has order'd for you
within, you fhall be well lodged, don't fear.

Alph. The Duke! what, what, what haft thou
got in thy head? What Duke, monkey, ha?

Maft. Sir, let me advife you, don't expofe
yourfelf; you are an old gentleman, and fhould
be wife; you are a little mad, which you don't
perceive; your friends have found it out. and
have delivered you over to me. (*Alph. fpits in his
face.*)——Say you fo, old boy?——A hey! [*Enter
keepers.*] Seize him here, and fifty ftraps o'th'
back prefently.   *Jul.*

Jul. (*afide.*) I'm afraid they'll make him mad indeed. (*They ftrap him.*)—Rare fport.

Alph. Hold, hold, hold, hold, hold.——Hark ye, gentlemen, gentlemen, one word, but one word: Pray, do me the favour to fhew me my chamber.

Maft. O ho! I'm glad to fee you begin to come to yourfelf, fir, I don't doubt, but proper methods will bring you to your fenfes again.

Alph. Yes, fir, I hope all will be well. Really I find myfelf at this time, as I think, very fenfible ——of fome ftrokes o'th' back.   (*afide.*)

Maft. I can fee your madnefs very much abated.

Alph. Yes, truly, I hope it is; though I can't fay but——a——I am ftill——a——little difcompofed.

Maft. There muft be fome time to reftore a man.   Rome was not built in a day.   But fince the Duke has fo much kindnefs for you, to be in hafte for your cure, when your next fit comes we'll double the dofe.——Here, lead the gentleman to his chamber: but he muft have no fupper to-night; take care of that.

Alph. Pray, fir, may I fleep?

Maft. A little you may.   In the morning we'll take 30 or 40 ounces of blood away; which, with a water-gruel diet, for a week or ten days, may moderate things mightily.——Go, carry him in, I'll follow prefently.

Alph. What a wretched dog am I!   Strapping for fupper, and water-gruel for breakfaft.

[*Exeunt Keepers and Alphonfo.*

Maft. You fee, fir, the Duke's orders are obey'd.

Jul. I'll not fail to acquaint him with it.   Pray let the old gentleman want nothing but his wits.

Maft. He fhall be taken perfect care of.—— My humble duty to his grace.   [*Exit Mafter.*

Jul.

Jul. So, now I think I have fix'd thee. This has fucceeded rarely !———I could burft with laughing now, lie down and roll about the room, I'm fo tickled with it. But I have other bufinefs to do; now's my time to ferve my miftrefs. Good ftars! guide me where fhe is, and I have nothing more to afk you, but a hufband; and that the fooner the better.   [*Exit.*

S C E N E V. *Near* Segovia.

Enter Seberto *and* Curio.

Seb. O'my confcience, we have quite loft him: he's not gone home, we have heard from thence this morning.

Cur. Faith, let's e'en turn back; this is but a wildgoofe chafe.

Seb. No, hang't, lets fee the end of thefe adventures now we are out : they muft end foon one way or other.

Cur. Which way fhall we go ? We have fcowered the champaign country, and all the villages, already.

Seb. We'll beat thefe woods ; and, if nothing ftart, we'll go to Segovia.

Cur. I'm afraid he's fick, or fallen into fome danger. He has no guide nor fervant with him.

Seb. Hang him, he's tough and hardy, he'll bear a great deal.

Cur. Shall we part, and go feveral ways ?

Seb. No, that will be melancholy ; let's e'en keep on together.   [*Exeunt.*

Enter

Enter Alinda *and* Juletta.

Jul. Indeed, madam, 'tis very cruel in you to shew this strange miftruft of me. Have I not always ferved you faithfully ? why do you fhun me thus ? What have I done to call my truth in queftion ? But I fee you are ftill doubtful; 'tis enough; I'll leave you ; and may you light of one will ferve you better. Farewel.

Alin. Prithee forgive me : I know thou art faithful, and thou art welcome to me ; a welcome partner to my miferies. Thou knoweft I love thee too.

Jul. I have indeed thought fo.

Alin. Alas ! my fears have fo diftracted me, I durft not truft myfelf.

Jul. Pray throw them by then, and let 'em diftract you fo no more ; at leaft confider how to prevent 'em. Pray put off this fool's coat; tho' it has kept you fecret hitherto, 'tis known now, and will betray you. Your arch-enemy Roderigo is abroad, and a thoufand more are feeking for you.

Alin. I know it, and would gladly change my drefs if I knew how : But, alas ! I have no other.

Jul. I'll equip you. I lay laft night at a poor widow's houfe here in the thicket, where I'll carry you, and difguife you anew ; myfelf too to attend you.

Alin. But haft thou any money ? for mine's all gone.

Jul. Enough for this occafion : I did not come out empty.

Alin. Haft thou feen Roderigo lately ?

Jul. This very morning in thefe woods. Take heed, for he has got a new fhape.

Alin.

Alin. A pilgrim's habit, I know it: was he alone?

Jul. No, madam: and, which made me wonder, he was in company with that very pilgrim, that handfome man you were concern'd you gave nothing to.

Alin. Is't poffible! Did they feem friends?

Jul. The greateft that could be.

Alin. Intimate?

Jul. Walk'd arm in arm.

Alin. What can this mean?

Jul. Lord! how concern'd fhe feems.

Alin. Canft thou fhew 'em me?

Jul. Not for the world, in this drefs: But come with me to my old woman's, and there I'll inform you further of the matter.

Alin. Let's be fpeedy then, for I'm full of agitation: Come, as we go, I'll tell thee all my fecrets.

Jul. I'll keep them faithfully.

[*Exeunt.*

End of Aɛt IV.

ACT

A C T V.

S C E N E I. *A Wood.*

Enter Roderigo *and* Pedro.

Rod. HOW fweet thefe folitary places are! how wantonly the wind blows through the leaves, and courts and plays with 'em ? Will ye fit down and fleep ; 'tis wondrous hot.

Ped. I cannot fleep, my friend ; my heart's too watchful to admit of flumbers.

Rod. The murmurs of this ftream perhaps may lull you into reft.

Ped. It is impoffible: have you feen no one yet ?

Rod. No creature.

Ped. What ftrange mufic was that we heard far off ?

Rod. I cannot guefs ; it was uncommon ; fometimes it feem'd hard by, at leaft I thought fo.

Ped. It pleafed me much : What could it be ? here's no inhabitants.

Rod. They talk of fairies, and fuch airy beings : If there are fuch, methinks they could not choofe a lovelier dwelling.

Ped. Thofe rocks, there, look like enchanted cells, form'd for fuch inhabitants. (*Mufic.*) Hark ! more mufic ! (*Mufic.*) Hark, gentle Roderigo ! (*again.*) O love ! what fuel's this to feed thy flame ? O Alinda !

Rod. (*afide.*) By all his woes, he weeps.

Rod. What are thefe ?

Ped. What !

I   *Rod.*

Rod. Thofe there; thofe things that com^e upon us : Did dot I fay thefe woods had wonde in 'em ?

Enter Alinda *and* Juletta, *like old Women.*

Jul. Now you may view 'em : there are the men you wifhed for. There they are both ; now you may boldly talk with 'em, and ne'er be guefs'd at. Don't be afraid : See ! they're fur-prifed ! they don't know what to make of us.

Alin. I tremble !

Jul. Then you fpoil all : Take courage and attack 'em. I'll bring you off, I'll warrant ye.

Alin. 'Tis he and Roderigo ; what peace dwells in their faces ! What a friendly calm !

Rod. They feem mortal : They come upon us ftill.

Ped. Let's meet 'em ; fear won't become us. Hail, reverend dames !

Alin. What do you feek, good men ?

Ped. We would feek happier fortunes.

Alin. Seek 'em, and make 'em.
    Tarry not, nor loiter here ;
    Here inhabits nought but fear :
    Be conftant, good, in faith be clear,
    Fortune will wait ye everywhere.

Ped. Whither fhould we go ? for we believe thee, and will obey thee.

Alin. Go to Segovia ; and there before the al-tar pay thy vows, thy gifts and prayers ; unload thy heavinefs.
    There fhed thy mournful tears, and gain thy
        fuit ;
    Such honeft, noble fhowers ne'er wanted fruit.

Jul.

Jul. (*to Rod.*) And next for you.
  See how he quakes !
  A secure confcience never fhakes.
  Thou haft been ill, be fo no more ;
  A good retreat is a great ftore :
  Thou haft commanded men of might ;
  Command thyfelf, and then thou'rt right.

Alin. Command thy will, thy foul defires ;
  Quench thy wild, unhallow'd fires,
  Command thy mind ; let that be pure ;
  A bleffing then thou may'ft procure.

Jul. Take fage advice : Go fay thy prayers ;
  Thou haft as many fins as hairs.
  Of lawlefs men, a lawlefs chief ;
  A rebel bloody, and a thief.

Alin. Retire, thou trembling guilt, retire ;
  And purge thee perfect in his fire :
  His life obferve ; be that thy guide,
  And heaven may then be on thy fide.

Jul. At Segovia, both appear.
Alin. Be wife, and happinefs is near.
Both. Be wife, and happinefs is near.
     [*Exeunt Alinda and Juletta.*

Rod. Aftonifhment ! what can this mean ?
They know my very foul.

Ped. Mine they've infpired :—Be wife and happinefs is near. Thofe were their parting words.
They had the awful found of facred truth, and I
have faith to comfort me. Come on, my friend.
The oracle enjoins an eafy pilgrimage. Let's try
what fate intends us.   [*Exeunt.*

SCENE II. *A Chamber in the Mad-houfe.*

Enter Mafter of the Mad-houfe, Seberto *and* Curio.

Cur. We have told you what he is, what time we have fought him, his nature and his name; the feeming boy too, we have given you, I think, a fair account of.

Seb. That the Duke fhould fend that letter, is impoffible; he knows him not. And for his madnefs, that we both can clear him of. A humourift he is indeed, a great one, violent too on every fmall occafion——but no more——

Cur. 'Twas fome trick that brought him hither; the letter and the page, both counterfeits: if therefore you'd be well advifed, don't keep him longer here.

Maft. Gentlemen, you have fatisfied me, and I'll releafe him: though I muft confefs, whether you call it madnefs or not, I believe a little more of our difcipline would do the old gentleman a kindnefs. But I'll difpute no longer—you fhall have him.

Seb Sir, we thank ye.

Maft. Here, bring in the old gentleman.

Cur. Poor Alphonfo!

Enter Keepers with Alphonfo.

Seb. Poor Alphonfo indeed! was there ever fuch a change! Sir, I'm glad once more to meet with you. (*To Alph.*)

Cur. I'm overjoy'd to find you.

Alph. Soft, no flights: paffions are all forbid here. Let your tongue go like a pendulum, fteady;

or

or that gentleman there will regulate your motion, with fifty ftrokes o' the back prefently.

Seb. There's no danger: you are fafe too; we have fatisfied the mafter, who, and what you are: and he has confented to releafe you.

Maft. Yes, fir, thefe gentlemen have affured me you are a fober perfon; fo I afk your excufe for what's paft, and reftore you to your liberty.

Alph. Very concife indeed: I am much beholden to you truly; and do confefs with great humility I have not deferved the favours you have been pleafed to beftow upon me. But if I have the honour to fee you at my houfe, I fhall not forget to return your bounty with fome ftrokes of acknowledgement.

Maft. Sir, your very humble fervant.

Alph. Sir, entirely yours.

Maft. Farewel, gentlemen.

Alph. Come, friends, one under one arm, and t'other under t'other: I muft make a pair of crutches of ye.——

Seb. You are very weak indeed.

Cur. You look wretchedly.

Alph. A little in love only, that's all. Ah Seberto. Ah Curio——fuch difcipline! the Lord have mercy on me. Had I been here 'till to-morrow morning, this dog would not have left me fix ounces of blood in my whole body.

Seb. Can you imagine who put this trick upon you?

Alph. The devil, to be fure; but who gave him his cue I can't tell——Come, carry me off: lead me to church, I'm in a very religious fit at this time, and will give fome thanks for my deli-very: when that's over, I'll be revenged.

[*Exeunt feverally.*
S C E N E

SCENE III. *Inside of a Cathedral with
an Altar.*

Solemn Music.

Pedro, Roderigo, *Governor, Courtiers, Ladies,
&c. discovered.*

Ped. For ourselves first thus we bend ;
Rod. Forgive us, heav'n, and be our friend.
 Accept our offerings we implore ;
 The peace, which we have lost, restore.
Ped. Give me Alinda, and I ask no more.
         (*Music.*

Enter Alphonso, Curio, *and* Seberto.

Alph. For my lost wits (let me see)
 First I pray ; and secondly,
 To be at home again and free ;
 And if I travel more——hang me.
         (*Music.*

Enter Alinda *and* Juletta, *like Shepherdesses.*

Jul. Here they all are, madam ; but fear nothing : the place protects you. My old Bilboa
master, o'my conscience. How in the name of
mischief got he out ? But they have pepper'd him
I see : that's some comfort.

Alph. I had a daughter once with just such a
young roguish leer as that : a filly too, that wait-
ed no her ; much such a slut as t'other. Are they
come to keeping of goats ? 'Tis very well : I
thought they'd never come to leading of apes.
            Alin.

Alin. (*Going to the altar.*) Thus we kneel, and
  thus we pray,
  Happiness attend this day.
  Hear me, heav'n, and, as I bend
  With faith and hope, some comfort send.

Jul. Hear her, hear her, if there be
  A spotless sweetness, this is she. (*Mufic.*

Seb. 'Tis she, sure.

Cur. 'Tis certainly.

Ped. Is it a vision ? Or is it she ?

Rod. 'Tis she, and what you were foretold, is
. now at hand. Rejoice, my friend, for happiness
attends you.

Ped. Now, Roderigo, I may stand in need of
your assistance.

Rod. My life is yours.

Ped. Then with a joy that lovers know, but
none else e'er conceiv'd, let me approach this
beauteous wanderer. (*Throws off his pilgrim's garb.*

Alin. O Pedro !

Ped. My life, my heaven.

Alph. Pedro : the devil it is ?

Gov. Noble Pedro ! are we so happy to have
you still among us ? This is an unexpected bles-
fing.

Alph. (*aside*) A very great blessing indeed.

Ped. In spite of all my griefs, life still prevails :
fate seems to have some farther business for me ;
if 'tis to wander on with fruitless care, and buffet
still with disappointments, let manhood be my
aid : but if the sullen cloud, that long has lower-
ing hung about my head, be destin'd to withdraw,
'tis the warm influence of your blessing, sir, that
must disperse it. (*Kneels to Alphonso.*

Alph. I bless thee !—Ha, ha :—Damn thee.

          Gov.

Gov. Sir, though I am a ftranger both to you and the requeft the noble Pedro makes you; his merit's fo well known to me, that I muft be his fecond in his fuit, and tell you nothing can e'er be in your power to grant, but his defert may claim.

Alph. I don't know what his defert may claim, governor: but, if it claims any thing but a gallows, he's a very impudent fellow.

Rod. Perhaps I being a mediator, fir, may change your thoughts to him— (*Difcovers himfelf.*

Alph. Roderigo!

Rod. Roderigo, fir, becomes a fuppliant for Pedro, that you would blefs yourfelf in bleffing him, and blefs him with the fair Alinda.

Alph. (*afide.*) Here's a dog for you: he finds the jade's a fcamperer, fo he has a mind to be off of the lay.——(*to Rod.*) Are you ferious in this requeft, fir?

Rod. Moft ferious, fir.

Alph. (*afide.*) I believe you may. Let me fee: he has a mind to be rid of her, why fhould not I? Pedro's a dog, and, if I could hang him, I would. But fince I can't, I'll be revenged another way; he fhall marry the gipfy.—— (*to Ped.*) Look ye, fir; and, madam, (*bowing to Alin.*) I have made fome fhort reflections upon the prefent pofture of affairs, and am come to a fhort conclufion. As to my bleffing, I can't conveniently fpare it you: but, if you can contrive to blefs one another, you may e'en be as blefled as you pleafe.

Ped. Moft generous Alphonfo.——

Alph. Moft courtly Pedro, you may fpare your compliment; for, if you take my word for it, the prefent I have made you, does not deferve it.

Jul.

Jul. But I fay, fhe deferves the whole world.

Alph. Hark you, madam; you had a Gillian once, nimble-chaps, I think we call'd her; pray, is this the lady?

Jul. No, fir, fhe's at home as you order'd her: I'm a little foot-boy, that walks at nights, and frightens old gentlemen, makes 'em lofe hats and cloaks——

Alph. And horfes too, ha?

Jul. Sometimes I do, fir, when the cafe requires it. I teach them the way too through hedges and ditches: and how to break their fhins againft a ftile.

Alph. A very pretty art truly.

Jul. Sometimes I'm a drum, fir; a drum at midnight. Ran tan dan, dra dan tan, fir; a page too upon occafion, to carry letters for the fecuring of old ftrollers.

Alph. Thou art the devil.

Jul. I'm worfe, fir, I'm an old woman fometimes.

Rod. Ha! that tells fortunes.

Jul. And frights pilgrims, and fends 'em to Segovia for their fortunes. I am mufic too, any thing to do her good. And now fhe has got her lover, I am Juletta again, and at your fervice, fir, if you pleafe to forgive me.

Alph. I dare not do otherwife, left thou fhoudft follow me ftill: fo I defire we may be friends, with all my heart; and, gentlemen, if any of you have a mind to marry her——

Jul. Sir, I am obliged to you; but I'm married to my miftrefs: with her I hope to pafs fome three or fourfcore years; at which time, fir, I fhall be

K

at your fervice; fo when you've any more pranks
to play, fir, you know where to have me!

Alph. 'Tis very well, I fhall be fure to fend to
thee.

Ped. One reconciliation more lies on my hands:
in which I muft engage the generous governor.
——Roderigo, fir, is not unknown to you; nor
is a ftranger to your intereft with the King: I
hope you will employ it to reftore him.

Gov. The King, indeed, is much incenfed;
but, when his merit fhall be laid before him, I
hope he'll find it eafy to forget his crimes: be it
my care to fet him right at court.

Alph. And mine to get home to my houfe again;
and if I leave it for fuch another expedition——
(*to Jul.*) May little nimble-chaps, here, be my
fellow-traveller.

Rod. And now, Alinda,

The dangerous tempeft of our woes blown o'er;
Safely we land upon love's peaceful fhore;
Unnumber'd bleffings now attend thy youth,
The fure reward of piety and truth.

> [*Exeunt omnes,*

F I N I S.

PLAYS printed for W. LOWNDES.

Juft publifhed, making 12 *handfome volumes in duodecimo, orna-mented with upwards of* 80 *Copper-plates, price* 2l. 2s. *bound, the common, or* 3l. 12s. *the royal fize, with prime Impreffions of the Plates, worked on French Colombier Paper.*

THE

NEW ENGLISH THEATRE.

Containing 60 of the beft TRAGEDIES and COMEDIES in the *Englifh* Language. Each Volume has an elegant vignette Title, and every Play a Frontifpiece, reprefenting ftriking Likeneffes of the moft favourite Actors and Actreffes, defigned and engraved by the beft Artifts.

*** Any of the Plays which compofe the *New Englifh Theatre* may be had feparate, price 6d. on common, or 1s. on royal Paper, with proof Plates.

The following Plays have been printed fince the firft Publica-tion of the *New Englifh Theatre*, and in the fame elegant man-ner:

Artaxerxes	Love in a Village
As you like it	Macbeth
Beggar's Opera	Maid of the Mill
Coriolanus	Meafure for Meafure
Cymbeline	Merchant of Venice
Foundling	Merry Wives of Windfor
Hamlet	Much ado about Nothing
Henry IV. Part 1.	Othello
Henry VIII.	Richard the Third
Hypocrite	Romeo and Juliet
Julius Cæfar	Taming of the Shrew
King John	Tempeft
King Lear	Twelfth Night—*and*
Lionel and Clariffa	Winter's Tale

The under-mentioned have lately been ornamented with new Plates, each containing an animated Portrait of Mrs. SIDDONS, all drawn by *Stothard*, and engraved by the moft eminent Artifts:

Fair Penitent
Gamefter
Grecian Daughter
Jane Shore
Ifabella
Mourning Bride

Venice Preferved
and

Mahomet—*and* ⎱ *with the Por-*
'The Orphan ⎰ *trait of Mifs*
Brunton.

PLAYS